'Night, Storyland

Library of Congress Cataloging-in-Publication Data

Corcoran, Mark
'Night, storyland
p.   cm.
"A Calico book."
Summary: A child at bedtime bids good night to favorite storybook
characters.
ISBN 0-8092-4351-2
[1. Bedtime—Fiction.   2. Books and reading—Fiction.]   I. Title.
PZ7.H141145Ni   1989
[E]—dc19   88-36797
                                                            CIP
                                                            AC

Copyright © 1989 by The Kipling Press
Text copyright © 1989 by The Kipling Press
Illustrations copyright © 1989 by Mark Corcoran
Designed by Tilman Reitzle
Art direction by Charlotte Krebs
All rights reserved
Published by Contemporary Books, Inc.
180 North Michigan Avenue, Chicago, Illinois 60601
Manufactured in the United States of America
Library of Congress Catalog Card Number: 88-36797
International Standard Book Number: 0-8092-4351-0

Published simultaneously in Canada by Beaverbooks, Ltd.
195 Allstate Parkway, Valleywood Business Park
Markham, Ontario L3R 4T8 Canada

'Night, Storyland

by

MARK CORCORAN

A CALICO BOOK

Published by Contemporary Books, Inc.

CHICAGO • NEW YORK

'Night, Three Bears

★

'Night, Tom Thumb

'Night, Peter Pan

'Night, Mr. Toad

'Night, Owl and Pussycat

'Night, Peter Rabbit

'Night, Pinocchio

'Night, Rapunzel

'Night, Robin Hood